DATE DUE

Forest Has a Song

POEMS BY

Amy Ludwig VanDerwater

ILLUSTRATED BY

Robbin Gourley

Clarion Books
HOUGHTON MIFFLIN HARCOURT
BOSTON * NEW YORK * 2013

Clarion Books
215 Park Avenue South, New York, New York 10003

Clarion Books is an imprint of Houghton Mifflin Harcourt Publishing Company.

www.hmhbooks.com

The illustrations were executed in watercolor.
The text was set in 14-point Godlike.
Book design by Kerry Martin

Library of Congress Cataloging-in-Publication Data
VanDerwater, Amy Ludwig.
Forest has a song : poems / by Amy Ludwig VanDerwater ; illustrations by Robbin Gourley.
p. cm.
ISBN 978-0-618-84349-7
I. Gourley, Robbin, ill. II. Title.
PS3622.A5947F67 2013
811'.6—dc23
2011052433

Manufactured in in China
SCP 10 9 8 7 6 5 4 3 2 1
4500391262

With love to my parents
Debby & George Ludwig
and my sister
Heidi Ludwig Zvolensky
—A.L.V.

For Hannah, Luke, and Jeff,
my companions in the forest
—R.G.

Invitation

Today
I heard
a pinecone fall.
I smell
a spicy breeze.
I see
Forest
wildly waving
rows of
friendly trees.

I'm here.
Come visit.
Please?

Dead Branch

Spongy springy stick.
I pick it into thin bits.
Slivers sail the wind.

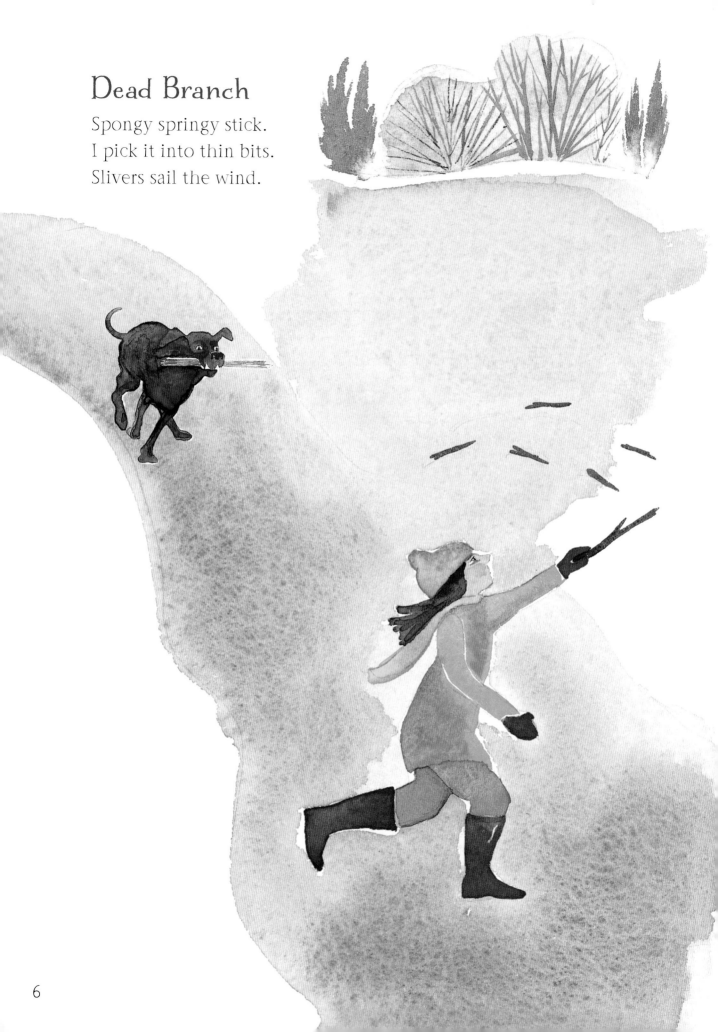

Chickadee

Come!
Fly here.
I have some seeds.
Fly here.
Sit on my hand.
I will not hurt you
Chickadee.
Fly here.
It's safe to land.

I'm watching.
I'm thinking.
I'm scared of you
Child.
I'm used to flying free.
But you are small.
Your hand is still.
Are all those seeds
for me?

Forest News

I stop to read
the *Forest News*
in mud or fallen snow.
Articles are printed
by critters on the go.

Foxes pass.
Deer run through.
Turkeys scratch
for hidden food.
Young raccoons
drink sips of creek.
Mouse and hawk
play hide-and-seek.
Here a possum
whiskery-wild
climbs a tree trunk
with her child.
And in this place
while people sleep
a rabbit hops.
A housecat creeps.

Scribbled hints
in footprints
tell about the day.
I stop to read
the *Forest News*
before it's worn away.

April Waking

Ferny frondy fiddleheads
unfurl curls from dirty beds.
Stretching stems they sweetly sing
greenest greetings sent to Spring.

Fossil

I dug in the creek bed.
I dug and I found
a grandfather fossil
asleep underground.
He whispered a story
of creatures in sand.
I listened as trilobites
filled up my hand.
For one flicker-minute
they tickled my palm.
Alive for an eye blink.
Forever dead calm.

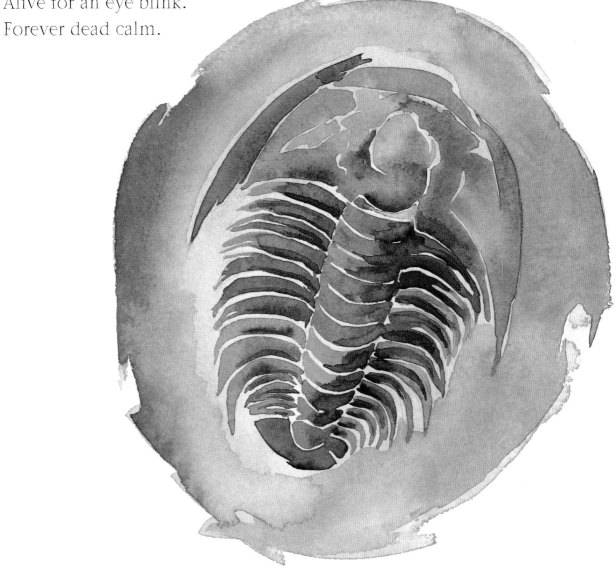

Proposal

Marry me.
Please marry me.

A tree frog calls
from tree to tree.
Hoping.
Hopping.
High above.
Crooning.
Plopping.
Finding love.

Pick me now.
Make me your choice.
I'm one great frog
with one strong voice.

Lady's Slipper

Were you at the Forest Ball?
Were you having fun?
When the clock struck midnight
did you have to run?
Did those footmen follow fast?
Did you hide from them?
Did you leave your silky slipper
balanced on this stem?

Forest Cinderella—
why?
You didn't even say
goodbye.

Spider

A never-tangling dangling spinner
knitting angles, trapping dinner.

Dusk

Sleep tight
baby animals
so small
so full of zest.

Burrow in a burrow.
Nestle in a nest.
Snuggle in a tree trunk.
Crawl beneath a stone.
Cuddle with a mama.
Huddle all alone.
Peek out at the sunset
winking way out west.

You'll meet the sun
with running fun.
It's night now.
Hush now.
Rest.

Lichens

Late at night I look for lichens
tracing flakes in shades of dark.

Messages in cursive code
cover stones and bumpy bark.

Lichens are graffiti artists.
Lichens make their mark.

First Flight

Mommy, I'm scared to be this high.
All owls are scared on their first try.

My tail feathers feel so tingly with fear.
You can do it. Calm down. Careful now. Steer.

I can't see a thing through all this black.
Just go to Spruce and come right back.

FLAP FLAP FLAP FLAP FLAP FLAP—WHOOOSH!
FLAP FLAP FLAP FLAP FLAP FLAP—SWOOOSH!

Look, Mom! I made it! Wow! I can fly!
I knew you could. You were born for sky.

Moss

Barefoot on this emerald carpet
toe-by-toe I squish across.
I softly sink in velvet green.
Oh how I wish for socks of moss.

Bone Pile

I wonder
were you someone's meal?
I wonder
were you old?
I wonder
did you freeze to death
last winter
in the cold?
I wonder
how you'd tell the tale.
I wonder
if you could.
I wonder
who will bury you?
I wonder
if I should.

Wintergreen

One bite of winter
lingers in a summer leaf.
Snowflakes fill my mouth.

Waiting for Deer

Quite quietly
I'm sitting here
nine minutes now
and
still
no
deer.

I look ahead.
I look behind.
I look around.
Again I find

no deer.

No deer.

No deer.

Surprise!

A fawn is
s-t-a-r-i-n-g
in my eyes.

Home

A rotten log is
home to bug
home to beetle
home to slug
home to chipmunk
home to bee
a lively living
hidden home
inside
a fallen tree.

Puff

Puff!
I found one.
Puff!
It's plump.
Puff!
Come see this
mushroom pump.
Puff!
It's spitting
spore on spore.
Puff!
I'm squeezing
more and more.
Puff!
Smoke scatters
summer air.
Puffball babies
everywhere!
Puff!

Warning

Poison
has three leaves.
Beware.

Ivy
climbs up trees.
Take care.

One green
touch can itch
so much.

Trust me.
I've been there.

Woodpecker

In a red cap
he types poems
with his beak
upon a tree.

hole hole hole hole
hole hole hole hole

  hole
  hole hole
  hole

    hole   *hole*
    hole   *hole*

Secretly
I'm hoping he
will translate one
for me.

Maples in October

They rustle to each other—

I think today's the day.
   Wind is getting colder.
Geese are on their way.
   Oak is throwing acorns.
It's time to go ahead.
   I think today's the day.
Let's change our leaves to red.

Squirrel

Tell me.
I promise not to tell.
I keep a promise very well.
Surely
you have squirreled a store
of nuts
beneath this forest floor.
I will not tell
one single soul.
Show me.
Where's your acorn hole?

Yes,
I've gathered gobs of treasure
all fall
but I never measure
How much
How many
Where it goes.
It's socked away for winter snows.
I have a stash from last September.
I'd show you.
I just can't remember.

Song

Under giant pines
I hear
a forest chorus
crisp and clear.

Winds whip.
Geese call.
Squirrels chase.
Leaves fall.
Trees creak.
Birds flap.
Deer run.
Twigs snap.

Silence in Forest
never lasts long.
Melody
is everywhere
mixing in
with piney air.

Forest has a song.

Snowflake Voices

I like to walk
outside
alone
in winter woods
behind my home.

I close my eyes
to softly hear
snowy voices
crystal clear.

Each silver
snowflake
sings my name.
Guess what?
No two sound the same.

Colorful Actor

Father cardinal
loves a wintry
wooded world
in brown and white.

Dramatically
he makes an entrance
through two birches
at stage right.

He plays his part
to no applause—
a freely flying
scarlet kite.

Farewell

Forest breathes
a spicy breeze.
It blows
into my ear.

When you go home
do not forget
my leaves
my song
my deer.
Remember
I am Forest.
Remember
I am here.